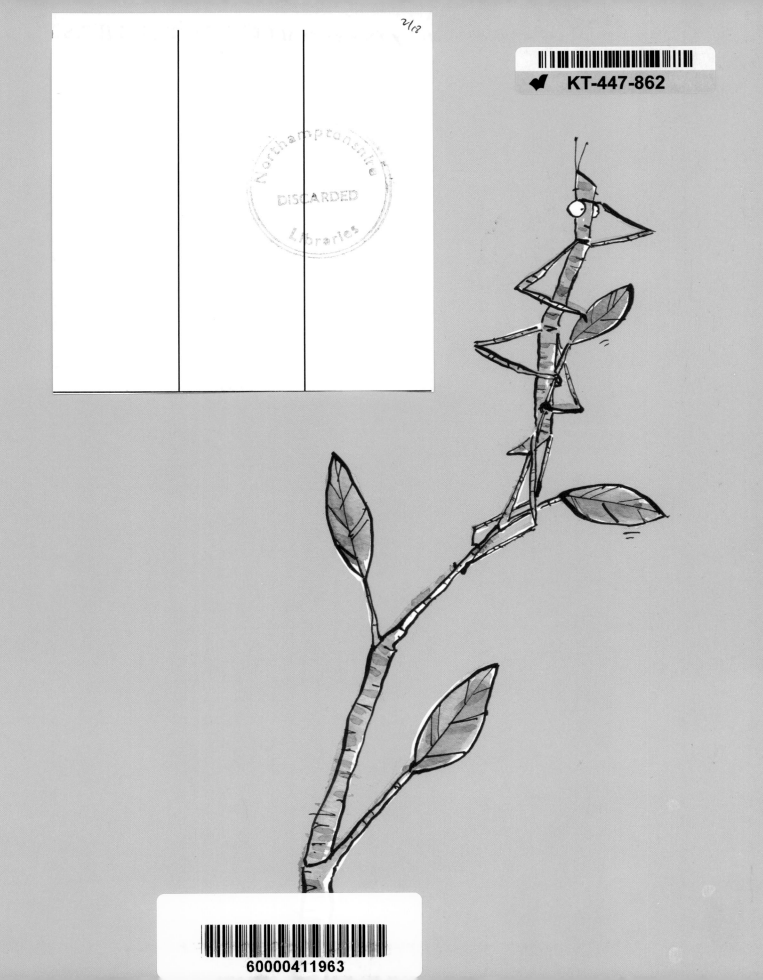

KT-447-862

Northamptonshire
DISCARDED
Libraries

60000411963

Northamptonshire
Libraries & Information
Service
CO

Askews & Holts	

For Mum and Dad,

Rafaël, Lucille and Marylène.

And Suzi for the best cloud.

With very much love

Bloomsbury Publishing, London, Oxford, New York, New Delhi and Sydney

First published in Great Britain in 2018 by Bloomsbury Publishing Plc
50 Bedford Square, London WC1B 3DP

www.bloomsbury.com

BLOOMSBURY is a registered trademark of Bloomsbury Publishing Plc

Text and illustrations © Chris Naylor-Ballesteros 2018

The moral rights of the author/illustrator have been asserted

All rights reserved
No part of this publication may be reproduced or transmitted by any means, electronic, mechanical,
photocopying or otherwise, without the prior permission of the publisher

A CIP catalogue record of this book is available from the British Library

ISBN 978 1 4088 6991 8 (HB)
ISBN 978 1 4088 6992 5 (PB)
ISBN 978 1 4088 8295 5 (eBook)

All papers used by Bloomsbury Publishing are natural, recyclable products made from wood grown in well managed forests.
The manufacturing processes conform to the environmental regulations of the country of origin

Printed in China by Leo Paper Products, Heshan, Guangdong

1 3 5 7 9 10 8 6 4 2

I love you, STICK INSECT

CHRIS NAYLOR-BALLESTEROS

BLOOMSBURY
LONDON OXFORD NEW YORK NEW DELHI SYDNEY

Tickle my splinters!
You are the most
beautiful
stick insect
I have ever seen.

Come with me and we'll have fun,
laughter and live happily
ever after . . .

We'll join a band, BANG on DRUMS and make some noise!

Then we'll **dip** our toes
into the bright blue sea.

We'll surf the ocean waves . . .

Skate arm in arm . . .

and fly away like birds!

So, come on,
take my hand
and together
we'll . . .

Race a speeding motorcycle
with the breeze in our feelers.

Enjoy all the fun of the fair!

We'll have a
huge cloud of
candyfloss . . .

And dance the hula –

whoopa-di-whoop!

Then we'll go to the movies and
share a big bucket of popcorn.

Just imagine –
me and you,
happily
ever
after.

Stick Insect,

I love y . . .

...ooooops!

... a STICK!

Why didn't someone
tell me?

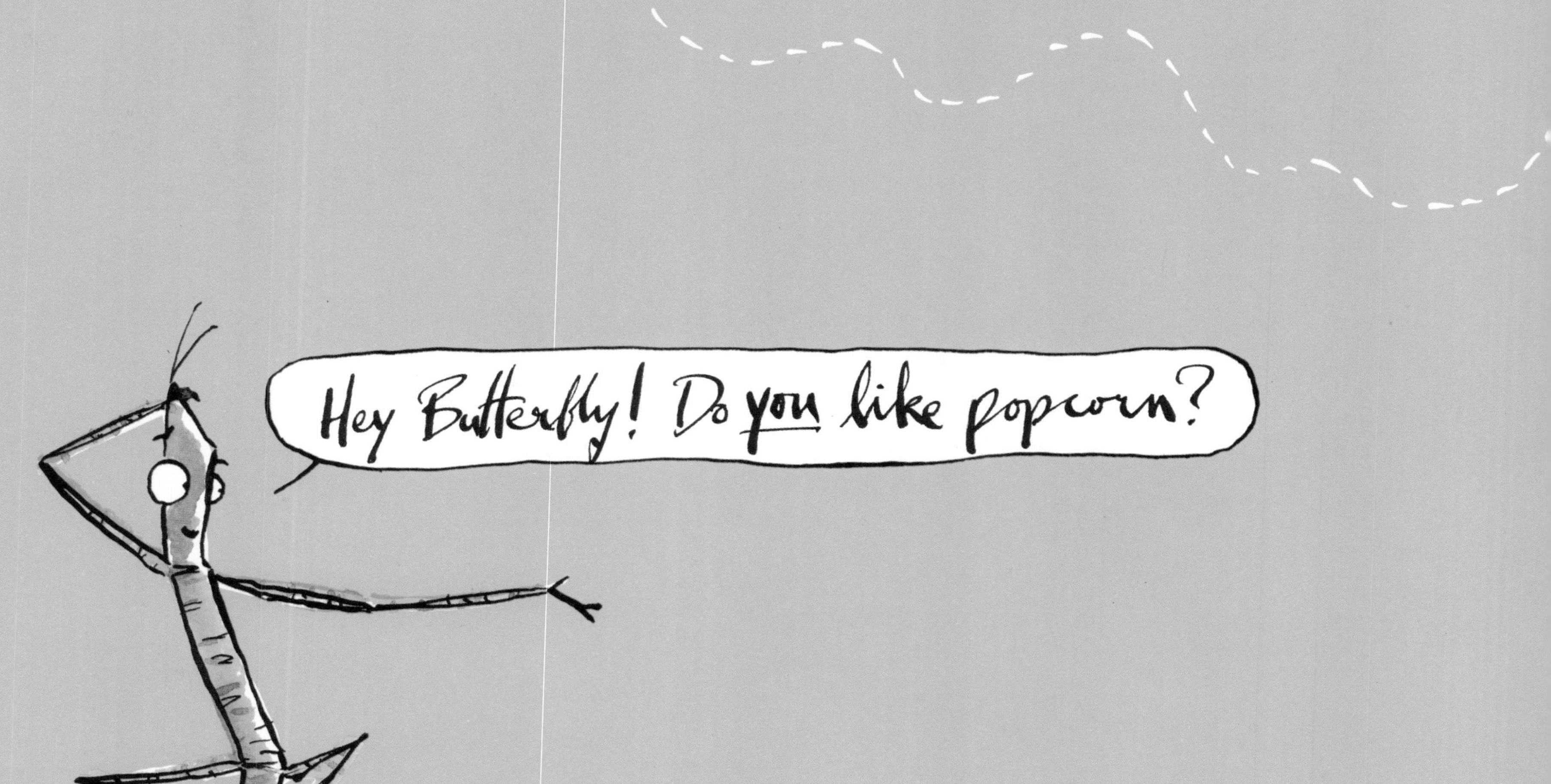
Hey Butterfly! Do you like popcorn?